P9-BYE-563

PRINCE OF A FROG

by Jackie Urbanovic

SCHOLASTIC INC.

For Emanuelle, my great-niece and a real princess

No part of this publication may be reproduced, stored in a retrieval system, or transmitted in any form or by any means, electronic, mechanical, photocopying, recording, or otherwise, without written permission of the publisher. For information regarding permission, write to Orchard Books, Scholastic Inc., Attention: Permissions Department,
557 Broadway, New York, NY 10012. • ISBN 978-0-545-86420-6 • Copyright © 2015 by Jackie Urbanovic. All rights reserved. Published by Orchard Books, an imprint of Scholastic Inc.
ORCHARD BOOKS and design are registered trademarks of Watts Publishing Group, Ltd., used under license. SCHOLASTIC and associated logos are trademarks and/or registered trademarks of Scholastic Inc. • 12 11 10 9 8 7 6 5 4 3 2 1   15 16 17 18 19 20/0 • Printed in the U.S.A.   08 • First Scholastic paperback printing, September 2015
The text type was set in Elroy and GFY Brutus. • Book design by Chelsea C. Donaldson

Once, in a faraway pond, lived a frog
named Hopper who loved to play.

He crooned tunes, but the fish thought he was off scale.

He kicked like a pro, but the ducks thought he was quackers.

Even the herons thought he was too odd to eat.

A prince is charming, brave, and loved.

Wow. How do I become a prince again?

With a kiss from a princess, of course.

At the edge of the pond, Hopper heard TAP-TAP-TAP-TAP-TAP coming from the treetops.

Across a distant field, Hopper smelled something gross.

Then, deep in the woods, Hopper found someone helpful.

P-S-S-S-T. I hear you're looking for a princess.

BAP!

Hopper kicked like a pro and the dog caught his flies.

Hopper crooned tunes and the dog howled in harmony.